DADDY'S PROBLEM

A short story to help children gain an understanding of addiction

AMAN PREMJI

ILLUSTRATED BY: MEGHNA SHARMA

First published in 2022 by AuthorsUpFront publishing services private limited
info@authorsupfront.com

Illustrated by: Meghna Sharma
ISBN: 978-93-94887-19-0

Special thanks to Vinitha, Jessica Guy,
and of course, my lovely mother, Hemali Premji,
for making this possible.

It's very nice to meet you, I am Anne!

My mommy Fran, says I look like her!

My daddy Dan, is a very frowny man.

Sometimes he gets mad and I hide until it's over.

He comes home at night, very bad-smelling.
When he gets hungry, then he starts yelling,
My Mommy tells him to go to bed,
Then makes him sleep on the sofa instead.

I asked my Mommy what was wrong with Daddy,
At first, she only looked at me sadly.
She told me Daddy is very sick,
That if he gets better, it'll be a neat trick.

She said it was because of his drinks,
They make him angry and he doesn't think.
"Is it my fault?" I asked, about to cry.
"Of course not, honey," she said with a sigh.

"Now go to bed baby, Daddy will be back soon.
If you wake up early you can watch some cartoons."
I went to bed but I woke up to shouting,
Daddy was yelling again, Mommy was pouting.

He said something loud, she said something back,
He raised his hand and I knew: I have to stop this attack.
I screamed and ran between them, scared of getting hit,
But then the yelling stopped and they
both stared at their kid.

Daddy fell to his knees, then he started crying,
He hugged me for long, until his tears started drying.
"I'm so sorry," he said, "I'll get better."
"It's okay Daddy, we can do this together."

So, Daddy went away to a place called rehab,

And two months later, he pulled up in a cab.

He stepped outside with a big, wide smile,

He looked so happy; you could see it from a mile.

221427

And now we are all together again,

We're going to celebrate me turning ten!

Every day is so full of laughter,

And it'll last forever after.

Aman Premji is an undergraduate at the University of Connecticut and is studying English. He hopes that this book will be helpful to anyone who needs it and he plans to write many more. In his free time, he likes to read, write, and play the bass guitar.